SEVEN
SUMMITS

DENALI

Ruth Daly

MEDIA ENHANCED BOOKS
AV²
BY WEIGL

The Great One

In a land filled with steep mountain ranges and snowy peaks, Denali rises higher than them all. From its base to its tallest peak, Denali measures 20,310 feet (6,190 meters) above sea level. Denali, also known as Mount McKinley, is the tallest mountain in North America. It is located in south-central Alaska and is part of a chain of mountains called the Alaska Range.

Denali has two peaks. Together, they are known as the Churchill Peaks. The South Peak is the highest and is the one most often climbed by **mountaineers**. Two miles to the north, the North Peak stands at 19,470 feet (5,935 m). It is no wonder that the name Denali means "high one" or "great one" in the Athabascan Alaska Native language.

Alaska's state flower is the forget-me-not. It is a common wildflower found around Denali.

Climbers usually take 17 to 21 days to make it to the top of Denali and back.

SEVEN SUMMITS

DENALI

Ruth Daly

www.av2books.com

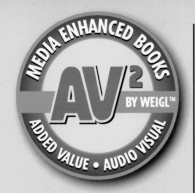

MEDIA ENHANCED BOOKS
AV2 BY WEIGL
ADDED VALUE • AUDIO VISUAL

AV² provides enriched content that supplements and complements this book. Weigl's AV² books strive to create inspired learning and engage young minds in a total learning experience.

Your AV² Media Enhanced books come alive with...

Audio
Listen to sections of the book read aloud.

Key Words
Study vocabulary, and complete a matching word activity.

Video
Watch informative video clips.

Quizzes
Test your knowledge.

Embedded Weblinks
Gain additional information for research.

Slideshow
View images and captions, and prepare a presentation.

Try This!
Complete activities and hands-on experiments.

... and much, much more!

Go to **www.av2books.com**, and enter this book's unique code.

BOOK CODE

AVL43844

AV² by Weigl brings you media enhanced books that support active learning.

Published by AV2 by Weigl
350 5th Avenue, 59th Floor
New York, NY 10118
Website: www.av2books.com

Library of Congress Cataloging-in-Publication Data
Names: Daly, Ruth, 1962-, author.
Title: Denali / Ruth Daly.
Description: New York : AV2 by Weigl, [2019] | Series: Seven summits | Includes index. | Audience: Grade 4 to 6.
Identifiers: LCCN 2019009582 (print) | LCCN 2019017855 (ebook) | ISBN 9781791114053 (multi User ebook) | ISBN 9781791114060 (single User ebook | ISBN 9781791114039 (hardcover : alk. paper) | ISBN 9781791114046 (softcover : alk. paper)
Subjects: LCSH: Denali, Mount (Alaska)--Juvenile literature. | Natural history--Alaska--Juvenile literature. | Mountain ecology--Alaska--Juvenile literature.
Classification: LCC GB525.5.A4 (ebook) | LCC GB525.5.A4 D35 2019 (print) | DDC 979.8/3--dc23
LC record available at https://lccn.loc.gov/2019009582

Printed in Guangzhou, China
1 2 3 4 5 6 7 8 9 0   23 22 21 20 19

052019
102318

Project Coordinator Heather Kissock
Designers Tammy West and Ana Maria Vidal

Every reasonable effort has been made to trace ownership and to obtain permission to reprint copyright material. The publishers would be pleased to have any errors or omissions brought to their attention so that they may be corrected in subsequent printings.

Photo Credits
Weigl acknowledges Getty Images, Alamy, and iStock as its primary photo suppliers for this title.

DENALI

SEVEN SUMMITS

CONTENTS

AV² Book Code 2

The Great One 4

Where in the World? 6

A Trip Back in Time....................8

Denali's Plants 10

Denali Wildlife...........................12

Early Explorers..........................14

The Big Picture..........................16

The People of Denali.................18

Timeline 20

Key Issue: Protecting
Denali and Its Park 22

Natural Attractions 24

Legends from Denali 26

What Have You Learned?...........28

Activity: Testing Permafrost......30

Key Words/Index 31

Log on to
www.av2books.com 32

The Great One

In a land filled with steep mountain ranges and snowy peaks, Denali rises higher than them all. From its base to its tallest peak, Denali measures 20,310 feet (6,190 meters) above sea level. Denali, also known as Mount McKinley, is the tallest mountain in North America. It is located in south-central Alaska and is part of a chain of mountains called the Alaska Range.

Denali has two peaks. Together, they are known as the Churchill Peaks. The South Peak is the highest and is the one most often climbed by **mountaineers**. Two miles to the north, the North Peak stands at 19,470 feet (5,935 m). It is no wonder that the name Denali means "high one" or "great one" in the Athabascan Alaska Native language.

Alaska's state flower is the forget-me-not. It is a common wildflower found around Denali.

Climbers usually take 17 to 21 days to make it to the top of Denali and back.

MAP OF DENALI

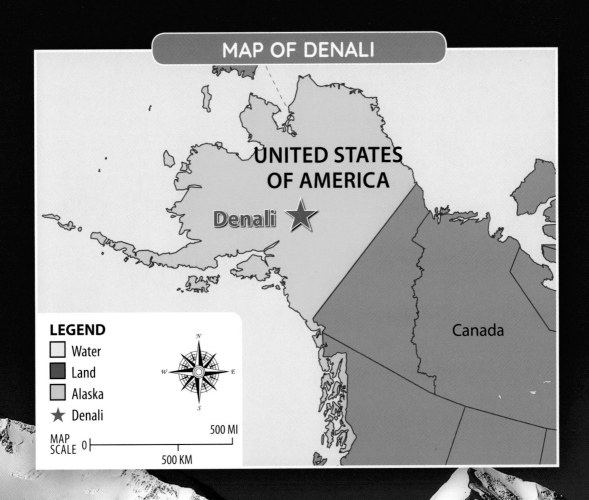

UNITED STATES
OF AMERICA

Denali ★

Canada

LEGEND
☐ Water
■ Land
☐ Alaska
★ Denali

N
W E
S

500 MI

MAP
SCALE 0 |———————————|
500 KM

DENALI FACTS

- Denali is contained within the Denali National Park and Preserve. The park was created to protect the mountain and the plants and animals that live around it.

- The name officially changed from Mount McKinley to Denali in 2015. The Alaska state government spent many years asking for the name to reflect what the Alaska Natives had called the mountain.

- When measured from its base to its **summit**, Denali is taller than Mount Everest, the world's highest mountain.

- Its height and arctic location make Denali one of the coldest mountains in the world. In the summer, the nighttime temperature can be as low as –40° Fahrenheit (–40° Celsius).

Where in the World?

Denali is located in the central portion of the Alaska Range, a series of mountains that form a curve through the state. The range extends for approximately 600 miles (966 km), dividing south-central Alaska from the **interior plateau**. Denali is about 133 miles (214 km) north of the state's largest city, Anchorage, and about 158 miles (254 km) south of Fairbanks.

Denali is so tall that it can be seen from Anchorage on a clear day.

The mountain sits in a remote area of Denali National Park and Preserve. The road closest to Denali is the George Parks Highway, which is 35 miles (56 km) away from the mountain's summit. People who want to gain access to the mountain usually rely on a combination of flight and foot.

The Alaska Railroad has a route that takes visitors to the entrance of Denali National Park.

Puzzler

The United States has 60 national parks. These parks have been established in areas that have unique landscapes, plants, and wildlife. Some states have more than one national park. Others do not have any. Alaska is one of the states with the most. See if you can match the following parks to their home states.

A. Yellowstone National Park

B. Everglades National Park

C. Sequoia National Park

D. Glacier National Park

E. Denali National Park and Preserve

F. Haleakala National Park

G. Acadia National Park

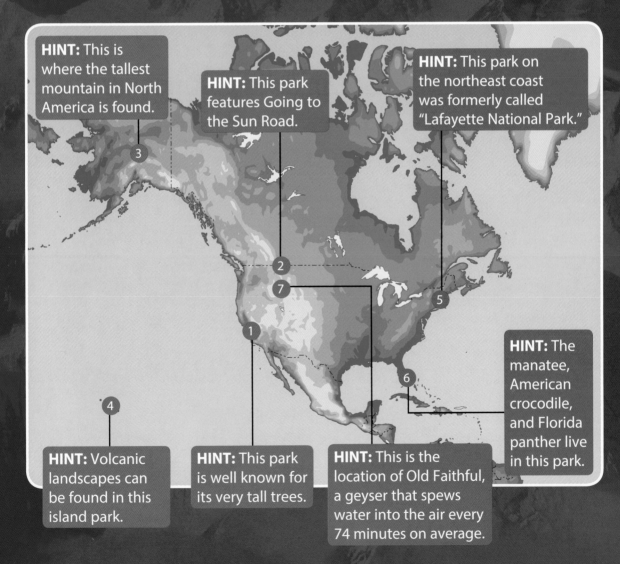

HINT: This is where the tallest mountain in North America is found.

HINT: This park features Going to the Sun Road.

HINT: This park on the northeast coast was formerly called "Lafayette National Park."

HINT: The manatee, American crocodile, and Florida panther live in this park.

HINT: Volcanic landscapes can be found in this island park.

HINT: This park is well known for its very tall trees.

HINT: This is the location of Old Faithful, a geyser that spews water into the air every 74 minutes on average.

A Trip Back in Time

The region in which Denali is located was once flat land. The mountains in the Alaska Range started to form approximately 65 million years ago along what is now called the Denali **Fault**. Mountains are formed when the plates that make up Earth's **crust** begin moving. In the case of the Alaska Range, the Pacific Plate and North American Plate began pushing against each other along the Denali fault line. This pushed the earth upward to create Denali and the other mountains in the Alaska Range.

This movement continues to take place. As a result, Denali continues to grow in size. Geologists believe that Denali is growing at a rate of 0.02 inches (0.5 millimeters) per year.

Denali and its surrounding range is made mostly of a type of rock called granite. Granite does not get worn away by ice as easily as some other types of rock. This allows Denali to keep growing taller.

Mountain Building

Earth's crust is broken into large pieces called tectonic plates. A river of hot **magma** flows under the plates. The movement of the magma causes the plates to slowly shift and push into each other. This pushing can cause the plates to rise upward. The scientific theory that describes how mountains form is called plate tectonics.

There are 12 large plates and many smaller plates. Each plate has a different shape and is 4 to 25 miles (6 to 40 km) thick. The Pacific Plate, which helped create the Alaska Range, is the largest tectonic plate. It is believed to cover about 40 million square miles (104 million sq. km) of Earth. Although mainly located in the Pacific Ocean, this plate moves in a northwest direction, sometimes bringing it into contact with the land-based North American plate. This contact contributes to the development and growth of mountains on the continent.

Tectonic plate collisions also cause earthquakes. Alaska experiences more earthquakes per year than anywhere else in the United States.

Denali's Plants

Denali's northern location limits the types of vegetation that can grow there. Due to its **altitude** and its cold temperatures, the upper portion of the mountain is covered with snow and glaciers year-round. This makes it impossible for anything to grow past an altitude of 7,500 feet (2,286 m).

At the lower levels of the mountain, however, a variety of plant life can be found. Evergreen forests known as taiga grow on the mountain's lower slopes. Trees here include spruce and aspen. Mosses line the forest floors, while shrubs grow in the open areas.

As the altitude increases, the plants become smaller. By about 3,000 feet (914 m), the climate becomes too cold for trees to grow. The landscape changes from taiga to brushy **tundra**. Plants that grow in these areas include tussocks of sedges, cottongrass, and the dwarfed shrubs of willows, alders, and birch.

Alpine meadows begin to appear at about 3,500 feet (1,067 m). Here, tiny plants, such as mountain avens, grow very close to the ground in the rocky landscape. The vivid blues, purples, and pinks of dwarf fireweed, moss campion, dwarf rhododendron, and forget-me-nots can be seen throughout the meadows.

TAIGA

TUNDRA

ALPINE MEADOW

Growing in Permafrost

Tundra areas have very short growing seasons. This is because much of the ground is permafrost. Permafrost is ground that has been frozen for thousands of years. A thin layer of topsoil thaws in the warmer summer months, allowing smaller plants to grow while the weather is warm. Over the summer months, more than 450 kinds of wildflowers can be found within Denali National Park and Preserve, along with several types of lichens, fungi, algae, and colorful mosses. The park also has a variety of berries, including blueberries and bearberries.

Plants that grow in permafrost actually help to prevent the land from thawing even more. The plants take in the energy from the Sun before it reaches the ground and makes the soil too warm.

Denali Wildlife

Denali is home to a range of wildlife. Some of the most common animals to see are bears, caribou, wolves, moose, and Dall sheep. All of these animals have specific **adaptations** that allow them to live in this cold northern environment.

The area is known for its grizzly bear population. The bears can be found hunting in the forests and foraging on the mountain tundra. They sometimes head to high mountain areas to **hibernate** in the winter. Hibernation lets the grizzly survive the cold Denali winters when food is scarce. Grizzly bears rely on berries and other animals for food. Moose, caribou calves, and snowshoe hares are just some of the animals they prey upon.

More than 170 types of birds have been recorded throughout the park. Due to the harsh climate, most do not remain in Denali year-round. One of Denali's few resident birds is the ptarmigan. These birds live in alpine and arctic regions of open tundra. Ptarmigan adapt to their environment by changing color in the winter, their brown feathers turning to white. This **camouflage** allows them to hide from predators, such as gyrfalcons and golden eagles.

Wolves in Denali usually live in packs of four to five wolves.

Dall Sheep

Dall sheep, also known as Dall's sheep, are often seen roaming the slopes of Denali. These sheep live in central and northern Alaska and other northern climates. They were named after William Healey Dall, a scientist who conducted surveys in Alaska in the late 1800s.

One of the most distinctive features of the Dall sheep is its horns. The rams, or male sheep, have amber-colored, curved horns. The ewes, on the other hand, have slim spikes similar to those of a mountain goat. A Dall sheep never sheds its horns. They keep growing throughout the life of the sheep.

Dall sheep can live in a variety of areas. However, in the summer, they often travel in groups searching for food, such as the roots of mountain avens. Dry, frozen grass makes up much of their winter diet, but in the spring they travel to high rocky areas in search of mineral licks. These are patches of soil that are high in mineral content.

A ram's horns will curl into a full circular shape when the ram is 7 to 8 years old.

Early Explorers

While the region's indigenous peoples have known about Denali for centuries, the first European to describe the mountain was English explorer George Vancouver, in 1794. The sighting inspired many **expeditions** to the mountain. Some people went to explore the area around it. Others wanted to scale its heights.

The first successful climb was clouded with doubt. Known as the Sourdough Expedition of 1910, it was comprised of a team of **prospectors** who had been mining the area at the time. Peter Anderson and Billy Taylor claimed that they had made it to the summit of the North Peak wearing homemade **crampons**. They said that they left an American flag and a 14-foot (4.3-m) spruce pole there, but no one believed them.

Three years later, another group decided to climb the South Peak. Led by Hudson Stuck, the climbers reached the summit on June 7, 1913. From that point, they could see the flag and spruce pole left on the north summit by the Sourdough Expedition. They were able to confirm the success of the 1910 climb.

George Vancouver traveled along much of the Pacific coast of North America in the late 1700s.

Biography
Charles Sheldon (1867–1928)

The founding of Denali National Park and Preserve would not have happened without the vision of Charles Sheldon. Sheldon was a hunter and **conservationist** from Vermont. Along with Harry P. Karstens, an outdoorsman and dog musher, he came up with an idea to establish a national park in the area around Denali.

When Sheldon arrived in 1906, he was amazed by the amount of wildlife present in the area. He became concerned that too many animals were being lost to hunters. Sheldon realized that the local **ecosystem** would be damaged if the **biodiversity** was reduced. He felt that creating a park would help to conserve the wildlife.

It took Sheldon almost 10 years to convince Congress to create Mount McKinley National Park. In 1917, the park was approved. The park was renamed Denali National Park and Preserve in 1980.

A marker in Denali National Park explains Charles Sheldon's role in creating the park.

The Big Picture

Denali attracts mountaineers whose aim is to climb the highest mountain on each continent. These mountains are known as the "seven summits." A second version of the list includes the highest mountain in Australia instead of Australasia. Mount Kosciuszko, in southeastern Australia, is 7,310 feet (2,228 m) tall.

Denali
North America
20,310 feet (6,190 m)

Mount Aconcagua
South America
22,841 feet (6,962 m)

Vinson Massif
Antarctica
16,050 feet (4,892 m)

North America

South America

Pacific Ocean

Atlantic Ocean

LEGEND
- Water
- Land
- Antarctica
- ▲ Mountain

MAP SCALE
0 — 2,000 MI
2,000 KM

N
W — E
S

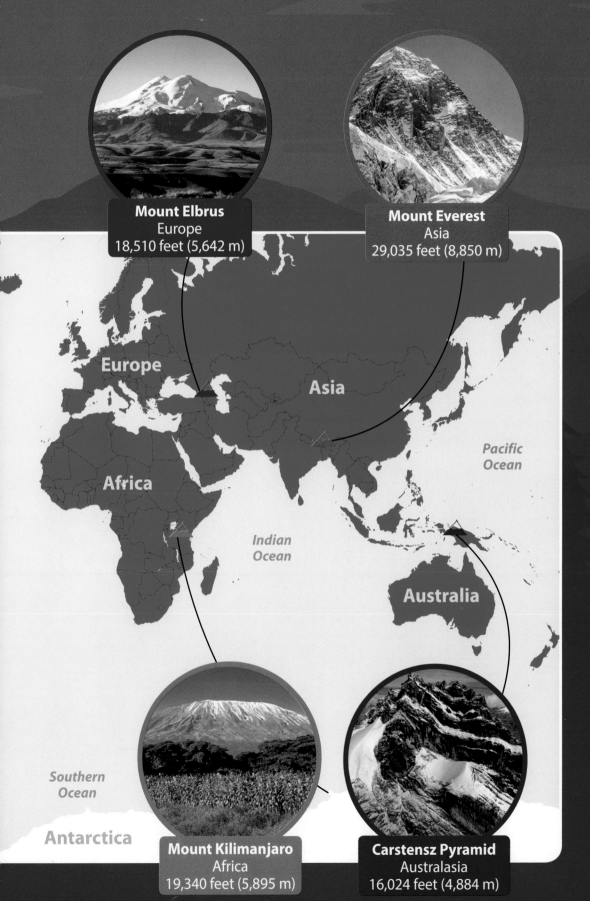

Mount Elbrus
Europe
18,510 feet (5,642 m)

Mount Everest
Asia
29,035 feet (8,850 m)

Europe

Asia

Pacific
Ocean

Africa

Indian
Ocean

Australia

Southern
Ocean

Antarctica

Mount Kilimanjaro
Africa
19,340 feet (5,895 m)

Carstensz Pyramid
Australasia
16,024 feet (4,884 m)

The People of Denali

For thousands of years, **nomadic** Alaska Natives known as the Athabascan people relied on the area around Denali for their survival. They hunted along the slopes and lowland hills of Denali for caribou, sheep, and moose. They fished in nearby rivers. They picked and preserved the berries that grew in the alpine meadows for the long winter months. When winter came, the tribes would camp lower on the mountain for protection against the weather. The Athabascan people believed that the mountain was a sacred place. They made sure to take from it only what was needed to survive.

Athabascan people remain in the area to this day. Many endeavor to keep Denali and its surroundings in a natural state. They work with the government to limit development in the area. The Athabascans want to preserve the ecosystem that has helped their people survive for such a long time.

Some Athabascans work as guides to share their culture and history with visitors to the area.

Athabascan Animals

The Athabascan people relied on many animals for their survival. Below are the Athabascan words for these animals. With a friend, try talking about the animals in Athabascan.

	ENGLISH	ATHABASCAN
	Moose	Dineg
	Duck	Nendaale
	Caribou	Ghinoy
	Grizzly Bear	Tsone
	Ptarmigan	Q'uyaldal
	Lynx	Nodog

Timeline

Prehistoric

70 million years ago Dinosaurs live in the region.

60–65 million years ago Mountains in the Alaska Range begin to form.

56 million years ago Denali begins to form.

5 million years ago Denali is only half its current height.

70 million years ago

56 million years ago

Exploration

1741 Russian explorers arrive on the land that is now Alaska.

1794 English explorer George Vancouver makes the first recorded reference to Denali.

1889 Frank Densmore, a mining prospector, names the mountain Densmore's Peak after hiking in its shadow.

1741

1896 Another prospector, William Dickey, names the mountain Mount McKinley, after presidential nominee, and later 25th president of the United States, William McKinley.

1903 An Alaskan judge named James Wickersham leads a team of four on the first attempt to climb the mountain. The group is unsuccessful.

1903 Frederick Cook claims to have reached Denali's summit. His claim is later proven to be false.

1896

1910 The Sourdough Expedition, made up of two prospectors, reaches the north summit, leaving a flag and a spruce pole behind.

1913 An expedition led by Hudson Stuck becomes the first group to reach the summit of the South Peak.

Development

1917 Mount McKinley National Park is established.

1917

1921 Harry P. Karstens becomes the first superintendent of the park.

1922 Construction of the Denali Park Road begins.

1947 Barbara Washburn becomes the first woman to climb the summit.

1980 The park is renamed Denali National Park and Preserve, and the Alaska Lands Act triples the size of the park by adding more land.

1922

Present

2005 Scientists discover dinosaur footprints in the park.

2013 Relatives of the four men who climbed Denali in 1913 participate in a commemorative climb of the mountain.

2013

2013 President Barack Obama signs the Denali National Park Improvement Act, which will allow for the construction of a small hydroelectric power plant and reduce the amount of diesel fuel used in the park.

2015

2015 A new, official height for Denali is established as 20,310 feet (6,190 meters).

2018 For the first time in 15 years, there are no climbing-related fatalities on Denali.

Key Issue: Protecting Denali and Its Park

National parks are designed to preserve a country's natural spaces. This includes the plants, animals, and landscapes found in the area. Land that has been designated as a national park is protected from excessive development. The priority of the U.S. National Park Service is to maintain as many of the country's natural areas as possible. Denali and its surrounding lands are one of the United States' most valued natural areas. It is important to the government that it remain relatively untouched by human activity.

When Mount McKinley National Park was renamed Denali National Park and Preserve in 1980, the park was expanded by approximately 4 million acres (1.6 million hectares). The expansion was meant to provide more protection to the land and the animals that live on it. While some areas have been set aside to allow local people to hunt, animals living within the park are now protected from poachers and hunters. Visitors to the area can view these animals in their natural **habitat**, and the animal populations can remain stable.

There are five popular mammals known as "The Big Five" in Denali. The caribou is one. The other four are the moose, the Dall sheep, the wolf, and the grizzly bear.

About 600 people are on Denali at a time during the main climbing season.

Still, visitors can impact the environment in other ways. The natural habitat can be damaged when too many people are present in a wildlife preserve. Fires can be started accidentally, trash can attract animals, and careless camping can destroy vegetation. In order to protect the park further, many campsites put a strict daily limit on the number of people permitted to camp. A road lottery limits the number of vehicles allowed to enter the park each year. A bus system for tourists also reduces traffic. Nearly 100,000 more people are visiting the park each year than they were 30 years ago.

SHOULD VISITORS BE ALLOWED TO EXPLORE DENALI NATIONAL PARK AND PRESERVE?

YES	NO
It allows them to appreciate and learn about Denali.	Denali should be treated as a nature preserve, not a tourist site.
Visitors are made aware of and may support conservation issues as a result of their visit.	Visitors require facilities that are not necessary in a wilderness area, such as hotels and stores.
Many visitors respect wilderness areas and work to limit their environmental footprint.	Some visitors damage vegetation and leave garbage behind.

Natural Attractions

Only a small percentage of the people who visit Denali National Park and Preserve go there to climb Denali. The climb itself requires moderate mountaineering skills, but the mountain's constantly changing weather can create very dangerous situations for climbers. Many visitors opt to climb and hike the park's smaller mountains instead. Mounts Foraker and Hunter, along with Cathedral Mountain, are all within the boundaries of the national park.

The park's wilderness setting appeals to people who crave adventure. Heli-skiing, ice climbing, dog sled demonstrations, and rafting on the Nenana River are some of the activities available to park visitors. The Eielson Visitor Center and the Murie Science and Learning Center provide information and activities about the history, geology, and wildlife of the area.

The rafting season in Denali is from the end of May to mid-September. The water is still cold even in the summer because it comes from the park's glaciers.

Climbing the Great One

Approximately 1,000 mountaineers attempt the climb up Denali every year. Only about half of these people complete the climb. There are more than 30 different routes for climbers to take. Each has its own unique challenges. The West Buttress, Muldrow Glacier, West Rib, and Cassin Ridge are four of the more popular routes.

West Buttress
The West Buttress is one of Denali's least challenging climbs, although it is known for its steep vertical **ascent**. Climbers on this route have to be careful of deep **crevasses** in the ice. They can cause serious injury to people who fall into them.

Muldrow Glacier
When Hudson Stuck's expedition made the first successful climb of the South Peak, they did so on the Muldrow Glacier route. For years, this was the most common way to climb Denali. Today, most people seeking an easier climb use the West Buttress route.

West Rib
The West Rib route travels along the south face of the mountain. The route is steeper than the West Buttress and includes sections of moderately deep snow as well as sections that have both rock and snow. Like the West Buttress, West Rib has crevasses along the route. Avalanches can also present danger to climbers.

Cassin Ridge
Climbers wanting a challenging ascent up Denali often take the Cassin Ridge route. Cassin Ridge is known for its mixed terrain, winding path, and steep sections of ice and rock. The route has very few escape routes, so climbers who experience difficulty are often at the mercy of the mountain.

Legends from Denali

The Athabascan people treat Denali with great respect. For them, it is more than just a very large mountain. Denali is a spiritual place that serves as a point of reference. They use the mountain as a guide and for hunting. Denali has an important place in their lives.

Many Athabascan stories revolve around the mountain. One legend explains how the mountain came to be. It tells the story of a young warrior who threw his harpoon at a giant wave. The wave turned to stone and became what is now known as Denali. Another legend describes how, a long time ago, magic stones were thrown into the air to protect the Athabascan people. The legend says that Denali was formed from these stones.

The name "Denali," or words with similar pronunciations, may have been used to describe the mountain for thousands of years.

Home of the Sun

The sheer size of Denali has had a great impact on the Athabascans. They see it as a powerful force in their environment. The story below is a demonstration of this belief.

Once, on the longest day of the year, a group of Athabascan hunters spent the day hunting at the base of the tall mountain known as Denali. They decided to make their camp that night on the south side of the mountain. That evening, they watched as the Sun disappeared into the mountain. In the morning, they awoke to see it come out from the other side. When they returned to their tribe, they informed the chief that they had most certainly found the home of the Sun because they had seen the Sun go into Denali in the evening and come out of it the next morning.

Denali can have up to 17 hours of daylight per day in the summer.

What Have You Learned?

True or False?

Decide whether the following statements are true or false. If the statement is false, make it true.

1 Denali is made mainly from limestone.

2 The South Peak of Denali is North America's highest point.

3 Grizzly bears can be found in forests and on glaciers.

4 Mount McKinley is located to the south of Denali.

5 The Denali people have lived close to the mountain for thousands of years.

6 Approximately 1,000 people attempt to climb Denali every year.

ANSWERS

1. False. Denali is made mainly from granite. **2.** True **3.** True **4.** False. Mount McKinley and Denali are the same mountain. **5.** False. The Athabascans have lived in the area for thousands of years. There are no Denali people. **6.** True

Short Answer

Answer the following questions using information from the book.

1. What name is Denali also called?
2. What are Denali's two peaks called?
3. Who was the first European to see Denali?
4. Whose expedition reached Denali's south summit first?
5. In what mountain range is Denali found?

Multiple Choice

Choose the best answer for the following questions.

1. **What does the word *denali* mean?**
   a. Wave of stone
   b. Home of the Sun
   c. The great one

2. **Who played a key role in founding the park that surrounds Denali?**
   a. Charles Sheldon
   b. Peter Anderson
   c. Harry P. Karstens

3. **What was the name of the route first used to climb Denali?**
   a. West Rib
   b. Muldrow Glacier
   c. West Buttress

4. **Approximately what percentage of people complete their climb of Denali?**
   a. 80 percent
   b. 30 percent
   c. 50 percent

Activity

Testing Permafrost

Permafrost covers much of Denali's tundra areas, allowing for only a short growing season. Permafrost stays permanently frozen unless heat or pressure is applied to it. You can demonstrate this principle using simple materials from the kitchen.

Materials

- Large pan filled with water
- Five identical ceramic coffee cups with bottom rims
- Hot tap water
- Ice water
- Small rocks (about 2 cups)
- Small sponge (for insulation)
- A freezer

Instructions

1. Fill the pan with about 1 inch (2.5 centimeters) of water. Place it in the freezer. Place an empty cup in the freezer, too. When the water is frozen, remove the pan and cup from the freezer.

2. Place the cold, empty cup on the ice. Fill another cup with ice water, and place it on the ice. Fill a third cup with hot tap water, and place it on the ice. Fill a fourth cup with heavy rocks, and place it on the ice. Fill the fifth cup with hot tap water. Put the sponge on the ice, and place the cup on top of the sponge. Be sure the cups do not touch each other

3. Put the pan with the five cups back into the freezer. After 15 minutes, remove the pan from the freezer. Remove all five cups from the pan. Feel the surface of the ice. Can you tell where all the different cups once sat?

Key Words

adaptations: adjustments made to suit an environment

altitude: height above sea level

ascent: rise or climb

biodiversity: the variety of plants and animals in a habitat

camouflage: a feature that allows an animal to blend in with its surroundings

conservationist: a person who is concerned about environmental issues

crampons: special footwear attached to climbing boots for travel over ice

crevasses: cracks in a glacier

crust: the outer layer of Earth

ecosystem: a group of living plants, animals, and their environment

expeditions: journeys with a special purpose

fault: a crack in Earth's crust

habitat: a place where plants or animals live and grow

hibernate: to be inactive over the winter months

interior plateau: a geographic region that extends across central North America

magma: hot liquid rock found under Earth's surface

mountaineers: people who climb mountains

nomadic: moving from place to place

prospectors: people who search for precious rocks or minerals

summit: the highest point of a mountain

tundra: a large area of land where the ground is frozen

Index

Alaska 4, 5, 6, 7, 9, 13, 20, 21
Alaska Native 4, 5, 18
Alaska Range 4, 6, 8, 9, 20, 29
animals 5, 12, 15, 19, 22, 23
Athabascan 4, 18, 19, 26, 27, 28

Denali National Park and Preserve 5, 6, 7, 11, 15, 21, 22, 23, 24

plants 5, 7, 10, 11, 22

Sheldon, Charles 15, 29
Sourdough Expedition 14, 20
Stuck, Hudson 14, 20, 25, 29

Vancouver, George 14, 20, 29

Log on to www.av2books.com

AV² by Weigl brings you media enhanced books that support active learning. Go to www.av2books.com, and enter the special code found on page 2 of this book. You will gain access to enriched and enhanced content that supplements and complements this book. Content includes video, audio, weblinks, quizzes, a slideshow, and activities.

AV² Online Navigation

Audio
Listen to sections of the book read aloud.

Video
Watch informative video clips.

Embedded Weblinks
Gain additional information for research.

Try This!
Complete activities and hands-on experiments.

Book Pages
AV² pages directly correspond to pages in the book.

Key Words
Study vocabulary, and complete a matching word activity.

Quizzes
Test your knowledge.

Slideshow
View images and captions, and prepare a presentation.

AV² was built to bridge the gap between print and digital. We encourage you to tell us what you like and what you want to see in the future.

Sign up to be an AV² Ambassador at www.av2books.com/ambassador.